But What If There's No Chimney?

By Emily Weisner Thompson and Mandy Hussey

Illustrated by Kate Lampe

INDIANA UNIVERSITY PRESS

Bloomington & Indianapolis

This book is a publication of

Indiana University Press
Office of Scholarly Publishing
Herman B Wells Library 350
1320 East 10th Street
Bloomington, Indiana 47405 USA

iupress.indiana.edu

Production date: June 2016
Plant location: Shenzhen Caimei Printing Co., Ltd.

Manufactured in China

Cataloging information is available from the Library of Congress.

ISBN 978-0-253-02392-6 (cloth)
ISBN 978-0-253-02393-3 (ebook)

1 2 3 4 5   21 20 19 18 17 16

Checkermint the elf is hiding inside!
Can you find him?

To Kendell, Zane, Elliott, and Maisie
E.W.T.

To John, Sam, Dylan, and Elise
M.H.

To Mom, Dad, Ben, and Will
K.L.

Checkermint

"I have a new job," said Ben's dad one day,
so they moved to a house with a big yard to play.

Ben loved his new home, but he had a new worry—
There's no chimney! he thought as the snow started to flurry.
"How will Santa get in?" he said to his dad.
"It's magic, my son. No need to be sad."

Ben wasn't convinced as he lay wide awake.
He turned to his dog, his furry friend, Jake.

On the bus the next morning, Ben gave Holly a frown.
"Without a chimney, how will Santa get down?"

Holly said, "I know! A magic key!"
But Ben wasn't sure just where one could be.

Ben sat at his desk and stared at the wall.
"What's wrong?" asked his teacher, Mrs. Hall.

"Magic!" he yelled. "And is there really a key?
How will Santa get in when we have no chimney?"
"I don't have a chimney," Mrs. Hall said.
"But Santa still visits if I stay in my bed."

I'll ask Santa; he seems pretty kind.
I'll write that big guy, I'm sure he won't mind.

Ben sat on his bed with his thoughts and a crayon,
"Dear Santa," he started, "I'm your biggest fan."

Outside Ben's window walked Mailman Fred.
Ben finished his note and jumped from the bed.
"Please get this to Santa—it's urgent!" he cried.
"I'm worried that Santa won't make it inside!"

Fred smiled and said, "No worries today,"
looking back at Ben as he drove away.
"Santa can use your dryer vent!" he called out.
Ben was puzzled. What was Fred talking about?

Later that day Ben's letter was dropped in a box,
mixed in with others seeking puppies and blocks.

Santa

Santa Claus
P.O. Box 1
Santa Claus, Indiana 47579

CLAUS

TO: SANTA

Box 1
Indiana

To Santa Claus, Indiana, with a
RAT-A-TAT-TAT!
picked up by an elf in a red and green hat.

Dear Santa,
I'm your biggest fan.
My house has
no chimney!
How are you
going to get in?

Love,
Ben

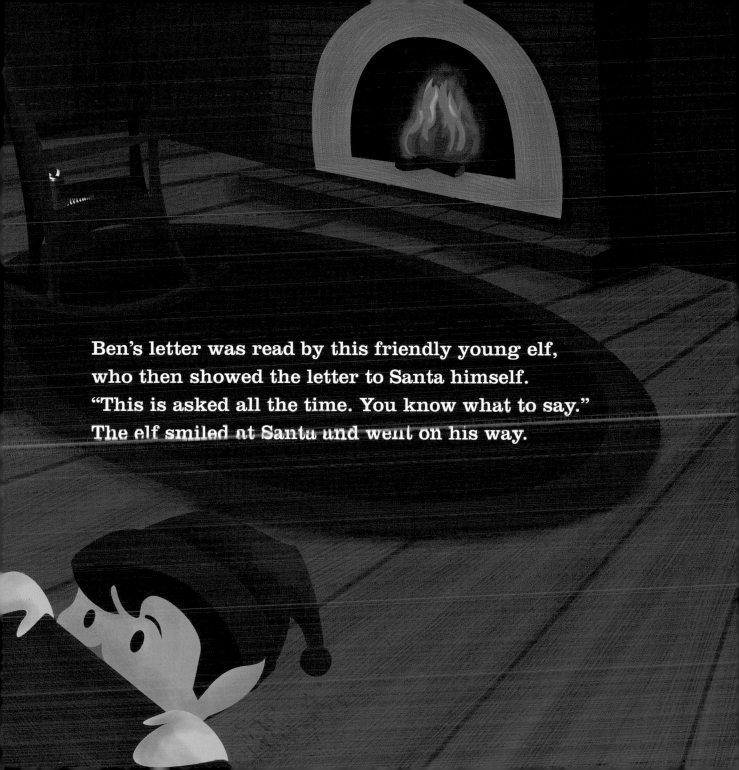

Ben's letter was read by this friendly young elf,
who then showed the letter to Santa himself.
"This is asked all the time. You know what to say."
The elf smiled at Santa and went on his way.

On Christmas Eve, Ben got Santa's letter.
He really hoped it'd make everything better.

He tore it open.
It started, "Dear Ben..."

Dear Ben,

Thank you for your letter. The Elves
and I have been hard at work preparing
for my journey. We hope you'll keep
the meaning of Christmas alive by
being kind and thinking of others.
Don't worry about the chimney—
didn't your dad tell you? I'm magic!
Believe.

Santa and the Elves

Ben's dad winked. "Santa's coming tonight!"
Ben smiled at Dad. "I knew you were right!"